Lightning Strikes

DONYA LYNNE

For intertwined with fear, we discover fearlessness.
—Author Unknown

COPYRIGHT

CHAPTER ONE

The only impossible journey is the one you never begin.
—Anthony Robbins

Rayna gulped past the lump in her throat as she peered out the windshield from the back seat. Crowds of partygoers decked out in everything from suits and slinky dresses to jeans and beach shorts packed the sidewalks lining Sunset Boulevard.

Crowds.

Packed.

The heel of Rayna's designer pump tapped a

panicked cadence on the floor. Was it too late to tell the driver to turn around and take her home?

The New Year's Eve party at the Mondrian hotel's rooftop Skybar was one of the hottest tickets in Los Angeles. Rayna should have been excited that her best friend had scored them a pair of tickets to such a prestigious event. Instead, she was on the verge of upchucking her lunch, and it felt like her nerve endings had turned to razor wire.

If she were normal, she would have been thrilled to mingle with Hollywood's elite. To see and be seen by some of LA's biggest, most powerful players.

But normal people didn't suffer from crippling fear every time they walked out their front doors. They didn't turn into a quivering mess at the thought of talking to strangers. They didn't think having their wisdom teeth pulled while undergoing a root canal and being massaged with steel wool would be preferable to entering a room with five hundred complete strangers.

Okay, so she wasn't *that* bad. Not anymore. She *used* to be, once upon a depressing time, but it had been years since she had reacted this badly to a social excursion that went beyond her safe zone of buying groceries, attending meetings with the family attorney, and taking her younger brother to one of his many doctor appointments.

Luckily, the attorney meetings had grown few and far between now that the lawsuits were settled, and Kai was well enough to drive himself to his own appointments. But for a while, Rayna had been forced to play chauffeur.

But even though her responsibilities didn't take her out of the house as often as they used to, hitting up Trader Joe's once a week to restock the groceries —as well as the avocado tzatziki dip Kai refused to give up when he wasn't training for the Special Olympics—wasn't the same as mingling among a crowd of the rich, famous, and notorious.

Rayna never went to parties. She never went anywhere socially, for that matter. And her inner DEFCON system was letting her know just how far outside charted waters she was by sending miniature earthquakes up and down her body.

Meanwhile, Amy was calmly touching up her lipstick in the seat beside her.

"You doing okay?" Amy pressed her lips together, then capped her lipstick and dropped it in her bejeweled handbag as their Uber slowed in front of the Mondrian.

"Yeah, uh-huh." She nodded nervously, tugging at the hem of the Dolce and Gabbana cocktail dress Amy had loaned her for the evening. The fabric was metallic gold with a bold, dark-red floral print that complemented her olive skin and black hair, but the dress showed a little more leg than she was used to.

The car stopped at the curb, and Amy opened her door. When Rayna remained glued to the seat, Amy halted with one foot on the pavement and one still in the car, frowning worriedly over her shoulder.

"Are you *sure* you're okay?" she asked.

Rayna gave another tight nod. "Mm-hmm, yep."

Her pulse raced, and the gremlins in her stomach were churning a deadly brew only a demon could love, but she refused to chicken out on her best friend.

Amy pulled her leg back into the car and turned toward her, leaving the door open. "Rayna . . ." She sounded both concerned and curious. "I thought you were better."

Rayna had thought she was better too. She hadn't had a panic attack in over nine months and had begun to venture out to new places, even going to the movies a couple of times without too much of a problem. So, why in the hell was she on the verge of going into a full-blown panic? She had known tonight wouldn't be easy, but she hadn't expected it to be *this* hard.

Going to this party and seeing it through was about so much more than just spending time with Amy, who she hadn't seen in over a year. Tonight was also about proving to herself that she was strong enough to overcome her fears. Again. Because this wasn't the first time she'd faced off against her agoraphobia. She'd defeated it once before. Surely, she could defeat it again.

Amy cocked her head. "Rayna, you look like you're about to faint."

Rayna swallowed and forced herself not to hyperventilate. "I'm f-fine, I just need a"—a wave of panic gripped her by the throat like a serial killer with a choking fetish—"a minute." She pressed her fingers to the base of her neck.

"She's not going to puke, is she?" the driver asked, peering into the rearview mirror.

"No," Amy said.

"Maybe," Rayna said at the same time.

"If she pukes in my car, you're—"

"She's not going to puke," Amy shot back before turning to Rayna like she was coaxing a scared kitten out from under a porch. "You're not going to puke, okay?" she said more calmly and reassuringly. "Now, come on, let's get you some fresh air. That'll help." She didn't sound any more convinced than Rayna felt, but Rayna took her hand anyway, and let her tug her toward the open door as she climbed out.

Rayna's palms were clammy, and a cold sweat had broken out on the back of her neck, but she managed to scoot across the seat and pull herself out of the Uber without losing the bowl of fruit she'd nibbled on that afternoon.

Once the car pulled away, Amy took both of Rayna's hands and squared her up in her sights like a concerned mother. "I thought you told me you were better."

"I am. I was." Rayna had been seeing a therapist for her agoraphobia for years, and she'd been making tremendous progress. "I haven't had an episode in months."

"Then what's wrong? Why now?"

"I don't know." Her gaze darted to all the lights, the glitz, and even a pair of sparkling sequined dresses that popped out from the sea of people on the other side of the street. "Maybe I'm freaking out because I've never been here before"—she glanced toward the hotel—"or because this is the first real test I've had since I left nursing school."

"You quit nursing school five years ago, Rain."

"Actually," Rayna said a little squeamishly, "it's only been four and a half."

Amy looked at her as if she were counting grains of salt. "Four and a half, five, who cares? Either way, it's a long time." Amy sighed, her eyebrows drawing together in a concerned frown. "I'm starting to worry about you, Rain."

Rayna recoiled slightly. "Me? Why?"

"Why?" Amy's brow rose high into her forehead, her baby blues opening wide. "This is why." She took a step back and gestured at her. "This . . . *panic*. I hate seeing you like this."

"And I hate *feeling* like this, but what am I going to do? This is my life now."

Amy's eyebrows scrunched and rose over the inside corners of her eyes. "I know, and I'm sorry, but it shouldn't have to be like this. What happened to your mom, and then your dad . . ." She sadly shook her head. "You shouldn't have to bear the brunt of that anymore. Certainly not like this."

"Yeah, well . . ." Rayna shrugged and forced herself to take another deep breath. "Not much I can do about it."

Amy knew all the tragic details of what had happened to make Rayna the way she was. She knew the hell, the pain, the suffering, all of it, because she'd had a front-row seat to the aftermath of her mom's disappearance, watching Rayna's trust in the world disintegrate in a matter of days, then bearing witness to years of struggle as Rayna tried to recover who she'd once been.

Just when Rayna had been making huge strides, even gaining the courage to go to college to become a nurse like her mom, tragedy struck again when her dad was killed in a horrible car accident.

He'd been driving Kai to the airport for a flight to New York, where Kai would train for the Olympics, when another car slammed into them. Dad died instantly, and Kai was left in critical condition. Not only did he suffer massive internal injuries, but the bones in his left leg had been crushed. They'd had to amputate while he lay in a coma, killing Kai's Olympic dreams with one slice.

When Kai woke four days later and saw that he only had one leg, he unraveled into a pit of depression so deep Rayna thought he was lost forever. It was like watching someone die while they were still alive.

She hadn't even thought twice about dropping out of college. Kai had been suicidal and required around-the-clock care. What other choice had there been? Mom was gone. Now their dad was too. Rayna became Kai's legal guardian, filling her parents' shoes, forced to grow up long before she was ready, attending to matters and responsibilities someone her age should never have to think about.

Maybe that was why her agoraphobia returned with such a vengeance. Not only had her father's tragic death and the loss of Kai's leg been a reminder of just how scary the world was, but she had also been overwhelmed by all the responsibilities she had inherited overnight. Running the household, tending to Kai, attorney meetings for the lawsuit filed against the kid who'd crashed into Dad's car. Then there were the court hearings, doctor appointments, interviews for in-home nurses, and about a million little unanticipated things that came up every day. For the first year, she rarely got a minute to just *be*.

So much shit got piled onto her shoulders in those first few weeks as Kai's guardian that her defenses crumbled, providing fertile ground for her agoraphobia to return. And not just return, but take on new life. Now she was back in therapy, trying to overcome her fear of the big, bad, scary world all over again.

"Oh, Rayna . . ." Amy sighed and pulled her into a hug. "I know life hasn't been fair to you, but I'm here if you need me. You know that. If there's anything I can do to help . . ."

"I wish there were," Rayna said, welcoming Amy's steadying embrace as she silently cursed her frail fortitude. "But I have to do it myself." She pulled away. "And I can." The self-assured nod she gave was more for herself than Amy. A feeble attempt to convince herself she could do the seemingly impossible twice in one lifetime. "I beat it once, I can beat it again."

Amy flashed an encouraging smile. "I know you can." She glanced behind her at the hotel, then looked back at Rayna like she was about to make a sacrifice. "But hey, if you're not feeling up to this tonight, we can go back to your house. Pick up a bottle of champagne on the way so we can make a toast at midnight. Grab a pizza or something. Put on our pj's and watch New Year's Rockin' Eve or a movie or whatever. You know, just keep it quiet and hang out, just the two of us, like when we were kids."

Rayna had to admit, that sounded nice. Comfortable. *Safe.*

But, damn it, she didn't want safe. What she wanted was to be the bold, spirited kid she'd been before her whole life had gone to shit.

Twelve-year-old Rayna had been fearless, tackling life like a boss. Twenty-five-year-old Rayna was afraid of her own shadow and couldn't even go to a damn New Year's Eve party without shaking like a frightened dog.

But Amy had gone to a lot of trouble to get these tickets. Rayna wasn't going to let them go to waste just because she was a little scared.

Okay, a lot scared, but whatever. She was doing this!

"No," she said, lifting her trembling chin, "I want to go in."

"Rayna, you don't have to—"

"I *need* to do this, Amy. If for no other reason than to prove to myself I can." She took a deep breath and blew it out, nodding once like she was putting a period on her barely existent courage, then glanced toward the entrance. "Once I get up there and get a couple of drinks in me, I'll relax. You'll see. It'll be okay." *God, please let it be okay.*

Amy studied her for a long moment, elegant and sophisticated in a yellow Versace dress that would have looked hideous on ninety-five percent of the female population, but it was absolutely stunning on her, with her lightly tanned skin and yellow-blond hair.

"You're sure?" Amy asked, her blue eyes piercing Rayna's.

No.

"I'm positive." She took Amy's hand and tugged her toward the entrance before she could have second thoughts. "Let's go."

Her legs might have been quaking, and her knees might have felt like gelatin, but she managed to cross the sidewalk in her strappy black-and-red heels without toppling over.

Less than two minutes later, she and Amy passed through the doors to the open-aired Skybar. The cloudless sky was their ceiling, the view of downtown

Los Angeles magnificent, the music being cranked out by a live DJ electric and alive.

And people. Lots of people. Lots of opportunities for someone with ill intent to grab her and make her disappear like her mom or do unspeakable things to her and—

She slammed her eyes shut and gave a tight shake of her head as if she'd shoved half a lemon into her mouth. She didn't need to be thinking shitty thoughts about being abducted and mutilated right now. That wasn't going to make being at this party any easier.

"Champagne." With an air of urgency, she pointed Amy toward a passing server carrying a tray of half-filled flutes.

They plucked a pair of glasses from the tray. Rayna downed hers in one swallow. If she didn't loosen up and stop seeing rapists and murderers in everyone she saw, this party would be over before it even began.

I'm safe, I'm okay. No one wants to hurt me. They're all just here to have a good time.

Affirmations went a long way to calm her down, but as she grabbed another glass of champagne, she had a feeling her affirmations were going to need a lot of help from liquid fortification if she was going to make it to midnight.

CHAPTER TWO

The Universe always strikes at your weakest point because that's what most needs strengthening.
—Chris Prentiss, *Zen and the Art of Happiness*

Cain Savage stepped onto his balcony and looked down at Skybar several floors below as he finished buttoning his light-blue linen shirt. The party was in full swing, music pumping, colored lights strobing and flashing.

He took out his phone and snapped a picture, then attached it to a text to his best friend, who'd flown to Portland earlier after getting a call that his sister was in the hospital for an emergency appendectomy.

CAIN: *Happy New Year. On my way to the party. Tell Lora I'm thinking about her and hoping she has a speedy recovery.*

He tucked his phone back into his pocket as his gaze swept over the mass of humanity milling around the pool on Skybar's upper deck, then he gazed out over the expanse of the city. The bumper-to-bumper traffic, towers of metal and glass in the distance, and the bright lights of LA were a stark contrast to the small Utah town he and Storm had just spent three months in.

He smiled at the change of scenery. This was what he loved about life on the road. Change was constant. If you got bored with where you were, a new town and new people were right around the corner to freshen things up.

Returning to the room, he slid on his silver Rolex, adjusted his cuffs, then shut off the light and headed for the door. Just as he stepped into the hall, his phone pinged with an incoming text.

STORM: *Looks like a great party. Drink one for me. Lora's doing great. They're holding her until morning, so I'll be staying at the hospital to celebrate New Year's with her. See you next year, man.*

Storm had attached a selfie with his sister, both of them all smiles, Lora lying in a hospital bed, flashing a tired thumbs-up.

It had always amazed Cain how alike they looked. Dark hair, brown eyes, same skin tone. For blood siblings, that wouldn't have been such a big deal, but both Storm and Lora had been adopted from different biological parents.

Storm—his real name was Mike—said his and Lora's similar physical traits meant they'd been destined to be brother and sister, and that being adopted by the same parents was just the universe's way of setting things right.

He'd always been a little woo-woo in that way, seeing the universe—or Spirit, as he sometimes called it—in everything.

Not that Cain didn't. Storm just took universal influence a little more seriously than Cain did. Like it was more of a religion or something, whereas Cain saw it as more like a guide.

Cain shot off a quick text that he would check in

with Storm tomorrow, then slid his phone into his pocket and made his way to the elevator.

Less than five minutes later, he stepped up to the open bar in Skybar.

"Gin and tonic," he said to the bartender as his gaze swept the clusters of women congregating nearby.

He wasn't necessarily out to get laid, but if the right woman came along, he wouldn't say no.

But that was the problem with LA. It was hard to find the "right woman" in this town. There was nothing wrong with ambition, but in Los Angeles ambition often turned into something ugly. People—women included—did a lot of questionable shit to work their way to the top of the food chain in this city, often becoming cutthroat, vindictive, and amoral just to get a step or two ahead of the competition.

Cain wasn't interested in a woman like that.

He also wasn't interested in the kind of woman who'd been created in a plastic surgeon's office, which ruled out three-quarters of the women at Skybar. He liked them real. Real lips, real boobs, real ass, with the ability to hold a real conversation, not one punctuated by commentary on the latest fashion trends, celebrity gossip, their next casting call, fake laughter, and the word "like" interjected every four seconds.

Which meant the pickings were slim.

Making them even slimmer was his disdain for gold diggers. He had no interest in bankrolling a woman's material needs, no matter how unbelievably gorgeous she was. Which was why he kept his identity a secret. If they knew who he was, every opportunistic, wallet-draining parasite would come after him like the bulls of Pamplona.

He lifted his drink to his lips, feeling more and more discouraged as he worked his way deeper into the room, surveying his options and coming up empty.

After ten minutes of milling, he started to think he was either going to have to lower his standards or spend the evening on his own. Then he turned toward the lower deck and his feet froze to the floor.

Everything about the woman he'd locked onto made his senses come to life like they'd been hit with a defibrillator.

Dark hair pulled up and out of her face, with loose strands hanging in relaxed curls over her slender neck and shoulders. Shiny red-and-gold dress that didn't cling too tightly to her subtle curves. Long, modelesque legs.

Legs did it for him, and this woman? She had stop-traffic legs.

She stood among a crowd, but far enough outside their circle that she appeared to be alone. Maybe even a little lost. Her gaze was directed out a nearby window as if she longed to be somewhere else.

Intriguing. Most of the women at the party seemed eager to be there. Eager to be seen, heard, offered a dose of E, a line of coke, or propositioned for a night with one of Hollywood's leading men, directors, or casting agents. But this woman? She reminded him of a tree he used to spend hours sitting under back home when he was younger. A magnificent, beautiful maple that grew in the middle of a meadow with no other trees around it, a little bit lonely, but comforting in a calming, nurturing way.

He didn't need to believe in signs from the universe to know he'd found his companion for the evening.

Taking a sip of his gin and tonic, he descended the handful of stairs from the upper deck and made his approach. He had to know why such a beautiful woman in such a crowded place looked so alone.

***

After two glasses of champagne and a turn around

the room at Amy's side, Rayna was feeling a little better, not quite as uptight and panicky. Her inner DEFCON had gone from a one to a three, but she wanted it to be at least a four before she attempted the kind of serious mingling Amy excelled at.

Amy could go to a party by herself and walk out with ten new friends. She'd already struck up conversations with two groups of starlets and one handsome stranger, and they hadn't even been at the party thirty minutes.

Rayna wasn't as outgoing and already needed a break from the sensory overload, so she had sequestered herself in the corner while Amy went to snag them a couple more drinks. While she waited for Amy to return, she would just stay tucked back here, away from all the noise, talking herself down from the ledge and—

"Want some company?"

She almost tripped over her own feet as she whirled toward the masculine voice coming from right beside her.

The man's eyebrows shot up as he took a quick step back, the hand not holding a drink whipping up in front of him, palm out. "Whoa, I'm sorry." He laughed apologetically. "I didn't mean to startle you."

Startle her? He'd crash-landed inside her four feet of personal space like an alien space cruiser. In her mental state, he was lucky she hadn't screamed for help.

She glanced toward the bar, searching for Amy's yellow dress. Unable to spot it through the crowd, she turned back to her uninvited guest . . . and damn near fell over her feet for a whole other reason.

Holy wow. He was hot. Like surface-of-the-sun hot. Zeus's offspring would be jealous. Hell, maybe he *was* Zeus's offspring. He certainly was demigod gorgeous enough. Blue eyes, trimmed beard, blondish-brown hair that was almost long enough on top to pull back in a ponytail but shorter on the sides. Kissable lips.

Very kissable lips.

"Uh . . ." Her hand fluttered back and forth nervously as she let out a sputtering laugh. "No, it's okay. I was just"—she pointed to her head —"thinking about something."

Thinking about something? Seriously?

Even to her own ears, she sounded lame. But she sure couldn't tell him the truth. That she'd been forcing herself to take what her therapist called mindful breaths. Breathe in for four, out for four. Then breathe in for five, out for five, and so on. It was a meditative technique she used to calm herself and bring her mind into the moment rather than let panic take her out at the knees.

He smiled, and her knees went weak anyway. He had the kind of smile that didn't just disarm her but stole her breath and made her heart skip a beat.

"Ah, deep thoughts?" he said.

She couldn't have looked away from him even if she wanted to. He was like a perfect sunset you didn't want to miss even a second of. "Something like that."

"My name's Cain." He held out his hand.

She eyed it, impulsively recoiling ever so slightly. She didn't mean to. This was just how she was, thanks to the phobia from hell. To her skewed sensibilities, an extended hand was a poisonous snake, not a polite form of greeting.

"I won't bite," he said with a disarming chuckle.

I wouldn't mind if you did.

She resisted smiling. Had she really just thought that?

With the image of him nipping her neck and shoulder slow burning it way into her brain, she gingerly took his hand. As her palm slid over his, a sizzling, slightly tingly sensation broke through her hand and up her forearm.

His palm was warm and dry, a little rough, but not in a bad way. More like a manly way. A man's hands *should* be rough. It proved he didn't sit on his ass pushing pencils all day. Not that there was anything wrong with men who held office jobs, but Rayna's sexual fantasies were dominated by men who didn't mind getting dirty from a little manual labor.

Stunned by the prickly sensation that was now creeping across her shoulder and into the back of her neck, she briefly lost her ability to speak, staring at him like he was some kind of magician. How else could she explain the satisfyingly warm sensation now working its way down her spine?

"And you are . . .?" he prompted, grinning as though he knew the effect he was having on her.

"What? Oh, uh . . . Ray—" Whoa, wait a second. Should she tell this guy her real name? What if he were some kind of stalker? "Renita," she lied. "My name's Renita."

A fake name was better. All the sexy wrapping paper and kissable lips aside, he was still a stranger. A hot stranger, but a stranger, nonetheless. And they didn't call it stranger danger for nothing.

He gave her a skeptical look like he suspected she'd given him a false name, then he just smiled, letting his hand linger in hers a moment longer before releasing it.

"Pleasure," he said, lifting his glass toward her in greeting. "Can I get you a drink, *Renita*?"

She glanced down at her empty hands. "Uh, no

thanks. My friend just went to get us—" She looked up just as Amy returned with a pair of cocktails.

"Who's this?" Amy asked, pushing her way between her and Cain like she was Rayna's self-appointed bodyguard.

"This is Cain." Rayna took one of the coral-colored cocktails from Amy and gave it a healthy sip. Nice. Fruity. But the burn of hard liquor as she swallowed told her the drink was anything but Kool-Aid. Thank God, because with he-of-the-blue-eyes looking at her like he wanted to do bad things to her —*good* bad things—she needed all the liquid fortitude she could get.

"I was just introducing myself to your friend." Cain held his hand toward Amy.

Amy looked from her to Stranger Danger, a.k.a. Zeus's offspring. Then her gaze fell dubiously to his outstretched hand as she arched one perfect, blond eyebrow. The expression was the same one Rayna's mom used to get with Kai, right before she asked him if he'd washed his hands after he whisked in and out of the bathroom between rounds of whatever video game he and his friends had been playing.

Amy glanced back at her, eyes narrowed suspiciously. "You're okay with this?"

Heat flooded Rayna's cheeks as her eyes dashed to Cain's. "I'm fine."

More than fine, because Cain was the most attractive man she'd ever laid eyes on. And *BONUS!* Upon his sudden arrival, she'd completely forgotten how unnerved she'd been at the thought of mingling only a few minutes ago.

Somehow Cain had taken her fear away rather than magnified it.

Most men had the opposite effect, raising her hackles and causing visions of abduction and sexual assault to dance in her head. But not Cain. He'd taken her mind off her shitty, fear-filled life completely. Something about that—about *him*—gave her hope.

Amy's wary gaze slid from her to Cain, then down to his hand before finally clasping it. "I'm Amy. I'm Rayna's best friend."

Rayna cringed as Amy gave away her lie.

"Rayna?" He tilted his head at her, arching one eyebrow as he smirked knowingly. "Not Renita?"

Amy threw her a suspicious look. "Renita? Did you tell him your name was Renita?"

If Rayna could have slinked away on her hands and knees while holding onto a shred of pride, she would. "Yes." She said it like she was scraping mud off the back of her throat.

"Why?" Amy swiped her hand from Cain's as if she'd just realized she was shaking hands with a serial killer. "Was he harassing you?" She threw him an accusing glare. "If he got out of line with you, I'll—"

"He wasn't harassing me. I just . . ." Her shoulders fell as she faced Cain. "I'm sorry. My name's not Renita. It's Rayna. I just, uh . . . I'm not used to—"

"You don't have to explain," he said, wearing an amused expression.

Embarrassment washed through her like dirty dishwater. "It's just that I don't get out much."

Why couldn't she be a normal person? A normal *woman*? One who wasn't constantly looking over her shoulder or planning for disaster? One who didn't see a rapist, serial killer, or murderer in every man she met, especially when the man was as fine as Cain and had chosen *her* to introduce himself to.

And how about that?

Skybar was crawling with gorgeous women, and yet Cain—a man who looked like he could get any woman he wanted—*had picked her*. She should be overjoyed. Ecstatic. Sending text messages to all her friends that a demigod had passed over half of the most desirable women in Los Angeles to introduce himself to *her*.

Instead, she was sticking her foot in her mouth every time she opened it.

"Well, you're here now," he said, his eyes kind and humored.

"And totally blowing it," she said with a pathetic laugh.

The small frown he gave her said he didn't agree. "I wouldn't say that."

If only she could start this conversation over again. "You're probably regretting saying hi to me right about now, huh?"

She said it jokingly, but she wouldn't have blamed him if he wrote her off as potentially neurotic and hightailed it to the other side of the bar to avoid her for the rest of the night. Which was why what he said next completely floored her.

"Actually, I couldn't be happier that I did." He eyed her for a moment over the rim of his glass as he took another drink, then gestured toward the dance floor on the upper deck. "Would you like to dance?"

CHAPTER THREE

Old friends pass away, new friends appear. It is just like the days. An old day passes, a new day arrives. The important thing is to make it meaningful: a meaningful friend or a meaningful day.
—Dalai Lama

Cain had definitely picked the most fascinating woman at the party.

Despite the third degree her friend had put him through, as well as the false name Rayna had given him—or maybe because of them—Cain was more intrigued now than he had been five minutes ago. Rayna obviously came with a juicy backstory.

Which meant he was ready to take this conversation to the dance floor, where they could get up close and personal and start working on chipping through those barriers she had up.

"Not so fast," Amy said, holding up her hand.

Well, shit. Looked like her friend wasn't done with him yet.

Amy cast Rayna a protective, somewhat worried glance, then snared Cain with wary eyes. "We need to know a little more about you before you drag Rayna off to God knows where."

He'd only asked her to dance, not go hiking in the woods in some remote area where it would be easy to hide her body.

Yep, Rayna *definitely* had a juicy backstory.

"Like what?" he asked.

"Like"—she took a moment as if considering where to start, then straightened her shoulders —"where do you live?"

"All over."

"All over?"

"I travel a lot."

"Are you saying you don't have a home?"

"Not really." He and Storm moved around so much that they kept a post office box in New York that Storm's dad checked every couple of weeks. He forwarded anything important to wherever they happened to be at the time. "I grew up in New York, but I don't consider that my home anymore."

"Okay, so where do you live right now?"

He casually lifted his eyes in the general direction of his room at the Mondrian. "Here."

The plan had been for him and Storm to spend a few days in Los Angeles, then head north to wine country for a month or two. Now it looked like they might be spending a few weeks in Portland with Storm's sister first.

Amy's eyes narrowed. "Here?" she said incredulously. "You're saying you live here? At this hotel?"

"For now. In a few days I'll be up in Portland."

"On business?"

"No. Visiting a friend."

"A friend?"

"My best friend's sister. She had surgery today."

"Oh." Amy appeared mildly chagrined. "I'm sorry. Nothing serious I hope."

"Appendectomy," he said dismissively.

Amy glanced at Rayna, who seemed eager for the interrogation to stop so she could have her friend's blessing and get on with her night.

But Amy appeared to be just getting started. "This *friend?* She's not a girlfriend, is she?"

"No. Just a friend. Storm would kill me if I asked her out."

"Storm?"

"My best friend. Lora's his sister."

"His name is Storm?"

Did all this really matter? But whatever, if this interrogation was what he had to endure to get time alone with Rayna, it was more than worth it. He couldn't explain what it was about Rayna that drew him in, but he knew without a doubt there was no way he was going to find a more interesting woman to spend the evening with.

"His real name is Mike," he said, "but I've called him Storm since we were kids."

"Why?"

He shrugged. "Because his last name is Sturm, and Storm made a good nickname."

"Oh." Amy swirled the cocktail in her hands, pausing as if she might have run out of questions.

No such luck.

"So, Cain, what do you do for a living that allows you to travel so much?"

He shrugged nonchalantly. "A little of this, a little of that." He was being intentionally vague, but he had no desire to reveal that he was the son and heir to a financial empire. He had left that title behind when he left New York and had no plans to return and claim it. Fuck his father and his billions. Cain had enough from his trust to live comfortably for the rest of his life, even if he never earned another dime from an honest day's work.

"A little of this and a little of that?" Amy questioned dubiously.

He sipped his drink. "Call me a jack of all trades."

Amy looked at him like she thought he was thick in the head. "Okay, then what are you a jack of?"

"Construction, hospitality, charitable work . . . and I can mix a mean cocktail if you stick me behind the bar." The short résumé wasn't the extent of his professional repertoire—not even close—but it made for a well-rounded sample.

"Is that all?" Amy's eyes narrowed, her tone doubtful.

"No." He got the feeling that she was asking if he was also into more illegal methods to earn an income, which he wasn't, but it would take him an hour to recount every job he'd held. He would rather spend that time getting to know Rayna, not passing some inquisition just to be able to talk to her.

"Then what else do you do?" Amy asked.

Despite his growing annoyance, he really didn't mind the third degree, because it meant Rayna had someone looking out for her. And every woman needed a friend who was looking out for her, especially at parties like this, where shit could go ten ways sideways for a pretty woman with one nefariously spiked drink. But even *his* patience had its limits.

"Look," he said as gently as he could, glancing from Amy to Rayna, "I'm a private person. I work hard to keep it that way. Not because I'm into unscrupulous shit or anything illegal, but because I believe in taking my time getting to know people and letting them get to know me." He softened his voice as he looked at Rayna. "And that's all I'm looking for here, just a chance to get to know you. I can assure you, I have no ulterior motives."

Rayna's cheeks flushed as a shy but hopeful smile spread over her dusky-rose lips.

Amy held up her hand like she was telling them both to slow their roll. "Well, Rayna's been through a lot, and I—"

"Clearly, she's been through a lot. Otherwise, you wouldn't be grilling me so hard just for asking her to dance."

Amy's face blanched, and she jutted out her chin as if she weren't used to being so politely put in her place. "Well, I'm just trying—"

"You're trying to look out for her, I get it." Cain glanced quickly to the side, setting his jaw, then breathed in and exhaled sharply, stepping forward.

"Okay, look, here's what you need to know about me." He was ready to end this discussion and get on with his night. "I'm an honest person. I work hard. I play even harder. I prefer wine to beer. I don't do drugs." He squared Amy up in his sights. "I don't sell drugs, either, if that's what you're worried about."

She lowered her gaze in a way that read all kinds of guilty.

He turned his attention back to Rayna. "I used to smoke, because I was young and stupid and thought it made me look cool. Now I know it just made me look as young and stupid as I was. But I do still smoke the occasional cigar, because, well, I like it." He shrugged unapologetically. "And I see nothing wrong with indulging in simple pleasures from time to time. I like simple pleasures. I think they're what life is all about. And I take pleasure where I can find it. That includes sex."

Rayna's face flushed a deeper shade of red as Amy inhaled a sharp but shallow breath.

He didn't believe in tiptoeing around the subject. It was clearly on Amy's mind, or she wouldn't have interrogated him so hard, trying to get at his intentions. And what better way to defuse someone's anxiety about something than to hit it head-on.

"I'm a single man," he continued with a no-nonsense shrug. "Of course I like sex. I think about it like everyone else does. I'll even admit that I've already thought about it with you." Rayna gasped, but instead of fear, he saw excited anticipation flash through her eyes. Given how the last five minutes had gone, her reaction was a little surprising. "But that doesn't mean I'm going to act on it," he quickly added, noting the flicker of disappointment that crossed her face. "That doesn't mean I can't honor the word *no*. I *can* control myself. I won't take something not willingly given. That's what little boys do. And I'm not a little boy. I'm a man, and men treat women better than that. *I* treat women better than that."

Rayna shyly tucked her chin as she exchanged expectant glances with Amy, almost as if seeking her approval but not quite. More like she was hinting to her friend to back off, because whether Amy liked him or not, Rayna planned on keeping him.

And that stroked Cain's ego more than he wanted to admit.

"I've been around the world twice," he said, pulling their eyes back to him so he could spill the rest of his pertinents. "My favorite city is Milan in the winter when there's a light snow falling. My favorite color is blue. My favorite food is anything made by Storm's full-blooded Italian mother. And, trust me, you've never tasted better bolognese anywhere in the world." He took a moment to let his eyes dance over Rayna's button nose, rosy cheeks, and full lips, which were parted as if she were a little breathless. Then he brought his gaze back to her large doelike eyes, which sparkled against the white twinkle lights strung around the bar.

She really was a stunning woman. The more he looked at her, the more beautiful she became.

He inched closer, pleased when she didn't back away. Lowering his voice and speaking more slowly—so she clearly understood that the words he spoke next were for her, and her alone—he said, "And I crossed the room to meet you, not because you're the most beautiful woman here—which you are—but because you are the only woman at this party who looks like she has something to say that I actually want to hear."

CHAPTER FOUR

When I let go of what I am, I become what I might be.
—Lao Tzu

Rayna's mouth fell open. Had she ever heard a more flattering compliment? She searched her memories and came up empty. Never. Not once had anyone curled her toes and lit her insides on fire with one sentence the way Cain just had.

Feeling like the sun had finally broken through the storm clouds that had been shrouding her soul for years, a smile so wide it actually made her stand up straighter broke over her face.

Could he be feeding her a line? Sure.

Did she think he was? Not at all. There was something pure about Cain. Honest. An invisible light that came from within that both soothed and excited her.

She motioned to an empty table by the window. "Would you like to join us?"

Amy turned warning eyes on her. "Rayna, are you sure you wa—?"

She cut Amy off before she could even finish her question. "Yes."

"But—"

She threw Amy a look that made her best friend snap her mouth shut.

"Thank you for looking out for me," she said pointedly, "but I've got this."

Amy's blond eyebrows popped up as if to say she was impressed with Rayna's sudden show of moxie. Then she nodded approvingly, a wry grin pulling at her mouth. "Okay then, you've got this."

Over the years, Amy had gotten used to looking out for her, running interference and designating herself as Rayna's protector. It was sweet of her to do, and Rayna was normally grateful for her efforts, but tonight? Right now? With Cain? Not only didn't she want Amy's protection, but she also didn't need it. For the first time in years—maybe for the first time *ever*—she had met a man who instantly made her feel safe.

With her last boyfriend, Shaun, it had taken weeks for her to feel comfortable being alone with him, and even longer for her to feel safe with him intimately. They'd dated for four weeks before she let him kiss her and four months before she had sex with him.

But what had taken weeks for Shaun to overcome had taken Cain less than ten minutes.

Feeling as breathless as if she'd just personally witnessed the unveiling of a priceless, never-before-seen Renoir, she squared her shoulders and straightened her spine as she turned back to Cain. She gestured toward the nearby table again. "Would you?" she said. "Care to join us, I mean?"

He glanced toward the table, then turned a heart-melting smile back to her. "I'd love to." He motioned for her to lead the way.

She felt his eyes on her as they crossed the short space, but instead of making her self-conscious, it made her feel decadent. Like Julia Roberts in *Pretty Woman* when she turned around at the bar in her black cocktail dress for Richard Gere to see her for the first time in something other than hooker clothes.

"Did you have a good holiday?" he asked as they took their seats.

She and Kai had spent a quiet Christmas at home, just the two of them. Then again, in her condition, any attempt to travel across the country to visit their grandparents would have been futile.

"Yes. You?"

He nodded. "I was in Utah for Christmas. Spent it with Storm and a family who runs a farm there."

"A farm? Like corn and soybeans? That sort of thing?" She sipped her drink.

He bobbed his head to the side, his expression wry. "Not exactly. So maybe 'farm' isn't the right word." He lifted his glass to his lips, seeming to consider a better way to describe the place. "It's more like the center of the community than a farm. They do have fields they tend to, where they grow hay and barley, but they also have a large vegetable garden and an orchard, as well as a huge pumpkin patch."

"It sounds like a big farm," Amy said, her focus split between Cain and scanning the growing crowd.

"It is. They provide produce to several national grocery store chains. But what they're really known for—at least to the locals—is their store and charity work." He relaxed in his seat as he continued. "Every day of the week, you can go into their little country store and grab the fresh produce that didn't get boxed and shipped out. And they use the fruit to make preserves, compotes, sauces, and the best apple cider this side of the Rockies."

"Sounds pretty amazing." If only Rayna could drive farther than a ten-mile radius from home, she would have loved to experience this family farm herself. And forget flying. Even at the height of her previous recovery, flying was off the table.

Before Cain could reply, a handsome man dressed in skinny jeans and a stylish short-sleeved button-down approached the table and asked Amy to dance.

Amy glanced between her and Cain. "You okay here?"

It was sweet of her to check, but Rayna was surprisingly relaxed. Cain had a strangely calming effect on her.

"Go on." Rayna made a shooing motion with her hand. "Go have fun. I'm fine."

Amy hesitated, then she sighed as if surrendering, gave her a smile and a wink, then extended her hand toward her would-be suitor as she uncrossed her legs and stood.

Poor sod. He probably thought he stood a chance. But Amy was off the market. She'd gotten engaged to her high school boyfriend three years ago. She now lived in Dallas where Andrew had taken a job at his dad's financial investment firm after graduation.

But that didn't mean she was a doormat at a hot party. She was loyal, but she had no problem dancing with a guy as long as he understood and honored that she wasn't interested in more.

With a wave behind her, Amy let the guy whisk her away to the dance floor.

"Is she always like that?" Cain asked after Amy disappeared into the crowd.

"Like what?"

"So protective of you?"

She glanced in the direction of the dance floor, catching a glimpse of Amy's yellow dress near the periphery. "It's a long story." She turned back to find Cain studying her with a mix of curiosity and wonder.

"What?" she asked.

The corners of his mouth lifted as his strong brow bunched gently over his nose. "Just trying to figure out what happened in your past to make you so . . . guarded."

Heat blasted into her cheeks as she ducked her head, looking away. "What do you mean?"

It was one thing to feel comfortable enough with him to already be fantasizing about what it would be like to kiss him, but something else entirely to know he could see her so clearly.

His soft chuckle drew her gaze back to him a moment later.

"You don't have a very good poker face," he said.

"Poker face?"

He lifted his ankle off his knee and shifted forward. "It's obvious there's a story here." He raised his drink in Amy's direction. "A reason why your friend watches over you like a hawk and cross-examined me as if I were on trial for crimes against humanity."

She groaned, her shoulders drooping. "I'm so sorry about that."

"Don't worry about it. I think it's good she's so protective, especially at a party like this." He gestured around the room. "But I have to admit, I'm extremely curious."

She glanced down into her half-empty glass. "It's a long story." She wasn't sure this was the right environment to get into that conversation.

"Yes, you said that." He leaned back and crossed his ankle over his knee again as he stretched his arm along the back of the seat. "And I'm not going anywhere anytime soon, so . . ."

Did he seriously expect her to open up about her

past just like that? So easily? When they'd only just met?

Her mouth flapped open, then clapped shut as she considered how much she should reveal, if anything at all.

As he got more comfortable and waited patiently for her to start talking, she couldn't help admiring how well he wore that shirt. Not only did it fit like it had been tailored just for him, but the blue brought out the color of his eyes. And the top two buttons were unfastened, revealing a nicely tanned neck adorned with a turquoise pendant strung on a strip of brown leather.

"Well . . ." she began. "I, uh . . ." She bit her lip.

She never talked about what had happened to her mom and the resulting mental and emotional derailment it had caused. But something in the way he was looking at her—so expectantly and with such patience and compassion—made her want to talk.

Before she was fully aware that she'd even begun to speak, she said, "Do you know what agoraphobia is?"

He shrugged and gave a contemplative shake of his head. "Isn't that like the fear of leaving the house or of open spaces or something?"

She pressed her lips together, not sure where her desire to open up to him had come from but already too far invested in the conversation to stop. "Sort of." Her hands intertwined on her lap, her fingers twisting around one another. "It's actually a fear of being caught in situations you can't escape. You know, where you can't easily get help if something goes wrong."

His chin slowly lifted with understanding, the wheels of his mind clearly turning. "Like being caught on a plane when you're having a heart attack."

"Yeah, something like that. But not necessarily that extreme. More like being in an elevator that breaks down. Or it could be as simple as not being able to take a walk around your neighborhood, or go grocery shopping, or—"

"Go to a New Year's Eve party?"

Her gaze shot to his. He was smiling, his expression knowing and sympathetic.

The knots in her neck and shoulders released, and she smiled back with a nod of capitulation. "Yeah, like going to a New Year's Eve party."

"I see." He studied her through narrowed eyes for a long moment. "Have you had agoraphobia all your life?"

Of course he knew she was talking about herself. It didn't take a master's degree in human behavior to figure that out.

"No. Just since—" She drew in her breath as her

heart skipped a beat at the memory of her mom. "Just since I was fourteen."

"That's a long time."

She nodded. "Eleven years."

He eyed her like he was receiving answers to questions he hadn't yet asked. "So, what causes agoraphobia, if you don't mind me asking?"

She looked down at her hands, feeling more exposed and vulnerable than she was used to. "It's different for everyone. Panic attacks. Drug use. Other phobias like claustrophobia. Traumatic events"—it always felt easier to hide her reason in the middle of the others when the subject came up—"There's this story about a guy who visited Alcatraz when he was thirteen, and he volunteered to be locked inside one of the prison cells. As soon as the door shut, he was cast into total darkness. A moment later, he heard a whisper come from right beside his head. 'You're mine now. Your soul is mine.' He's in his forties now, but to this day, he can't be in the dark. He can't go anywhere that could be dark, like a movie theater or a haunted house. He can't sleep in a dark room or travel at night." She shrugged. "That's a form of agoraphobia that was caused by a traumatic event and enhanced by another phobia: fear of the dark. But other things that can cause it are bad relationships, abuse, being the victim of a crime. You know, stuff like that."

She'd done a lot of reading about her condition over the years. Comparatively speaking, her case wasn't as bad as others. At least she could sleep in a room at night with the lights off.

"Which was it for you?" Cain asked with an air of caution.

She took a hasty drink of her cocktail. "Traumatic event," she said softly. "My mom disappeared when I was fourteen."

"Disappeared?"

"She left to drive cross-country to visit her parents for the holidays, and we never saw her again." She made it sound so matter of fact, but the loss had been anything but. It still was.

"What happened?"

"I wish I knew." The lump that always formed in her throat when she thought about her mom threatened to cut off her voice, but she managed to work her way around it. "She just vanished."

"Vanished?" His expression pinched into a horrified scowl. "How does someone just vanish?"

Another shrug. "Again, I wish I knew. We've considered everything. *Everything*," she repeated for emphasis. "Even alien abduction, if you can believe that." She laughed pathetically at herself and glanced out into the growing crowd, catching sight of Amy laughing and dancing near the DJ booth. "But the truth is probably more realistic and a lot uglier, so . . ." She lowered her gaze, not wanting to think about the more likely options she'd come up over the years with for her mom's disappearance.

He gently took her hand. "I'm so sorry. If you don't want to talk about this, I completely understand."

"No, it's okay. I, uh . . ." She let out an awkward laugh, like she knew how odd it was to be opening up to a complete stranger. But she couldn't help herself, because he didn't feel like a stranger. He felt like a dear friend she hadn't seen for a while. "Actually, it feels good to talk about it to you."

His fingers squeezed hers reassuringly, and he smiled like she'd just paid him a high compliment.

"You're easy to talk to," she said before glancing down at their joined hands. Cain was like a lighthouse guiding her safely to shore. The buoy keeping her afloat on stormy water. She'd never felt so safe with someone she'd just met, but there was no denying their connection. "Has anyone ever told you that?"

"Once or twice," he said, a sparkle in his eyes.

Of course they had.

She fought the shy smile trying to break over her

face, looked away, and continued, "After it happened, I could barely leave my house for weeks. I couldn't even go to school at first. I had to be tutored at home. When I got well enough to return to classes, the other kids looked at me like I'd become a freak. I easily got scared and would sometimes have these . . . *episodes* in class. Panic attacks. Really bad ones. Something would trigger my fear, and I'd freak out, right there in math class or in the lunchroom or wherever. It was so humiliating."

"I can imagine." His thumb caressed the back of her hand. "How did you cope?"

"For a while, I didn't. I just wanted to make it through the day, then the next day, and the next day." Those first few months after her mom vanished were the worst, and there had been days she'd thought she would never get her life back. "But then I started seeing a therapist"—she huffed out a caustic laugh—"which made me even more of a weirdo to my classmates. But whatever, after I started talking to a therapist, I started getting better. That's when I learned that my condition had a name, and, somehow, that gave me hope."

"Knowledge is power?" he asked, shifting closer.

She grinned. "Yeah, I guess." She glanced down at their joined hands again. His was tanner than hers, more rugged. The hand of a man who worked hard for a living. "You've got nice hands," she said without thinking.

The moment she said it, her face blazed hot. *You've got nice hands?* Where had that come from?

"Thank you," he said as easily as if she'd complimented his shirt. He shifted his hold on her fingers to stroke his thumb over her knuckles. "So do you. They're soft."

Catching the inside of her bottom lip between her teeth, she stared at his thumb as it caressed back and forth, sending a mildly pleasant sizzling sensation up her arm.

A little breathless and a lot more aware of how close he was, she inhaled deeply, then slowly blew it out as she met his gaze again. "So, um . . . where was I?"

He was making it hard for her to think.

"Knowledge is power," he said.

"Oh, yes. Therapy." She took a deep breath, more to keep her emotions in check as the arousal he was stirring to life inside her magnified with each thumbstroke and inhale of his mild cologne. "Once I started therapy and learned about my condition, I got better. I was finally able to leave the house without falling apart, and I started having fewer panic attacks. I improved so much that I was actually able to go to college, which I'd begun to think I wouldn't be possible when things were at their worst."

Cain shifted in his seat, his expression acutely focused like he'd been digesting every word and working them over in his mind. "So, if you got better, why is tonight so hard? What changed?"

"Everything." She smiled dismally and shook her head at how her world had come crashing back down a year later. "My dad and little brother were in a horrible accident. My dad was killed. And Kai—my brother—almost died."

Shocked eyes stared back at her. "Oh my God, Rayna . . ."

Like the story about her mom, she hardly ever talked about their accident, but Cain made it so easy.

"Why are you so easy to talk to?" she said with an awkward laugh. "I mean, I never talk about this. To anyone. And I'm talking to you about it. And we only just met. Is this crazy? Am I insane?" She laughed again, shaking her head as she buried her face in her palm.

He chuckled modestly, scooting closer. "You're not insane. Maybe I just put out good-listener vibes or something."

She peered up at him. "Good-listener vibes?"

He held up his free hand like he was innocent. "Hey, I don't know." He dropped his hand to his thigh, then leaned back and tilted his head thoughtfully. "Or maybe it's like I said earlier, you really *are* the only woman here who has something to say worth listening to. Maybe you're picking up on that."

She rolled her eyes good-naturedly. "Oh, come on. You can't honestly say you wanted to hear about my parents' deaths and how it caused me to have agoraphobia."

"Why not?"

Her mouth fell open. "Well . . . because . . ."

He raised his eyebrows expectantly, waiting for her to continue.

"Well, it's macabre."

"It's not macabre," he said with a gentle laugh, letting his fingers intertwine easily with hers. "It's your life." He shrugged. "It's you. It's who you are and why you're the way you are. It's your history. What's more interesting than that?"

Was Cain for real? Was he really interested in hearing about her depressing past and how it had affected her?

Warmth crept into her chest and up her neck, and she lowered her head. "I wasn't lying when I said I don't normally talk about this stuff."

"If you want to stop, feel free to change the

subject. But don't do it because you think you're boring me or because—"

"*Am* I boring you?" she asked with a precarious smile.

He tilted his head as if she couldn't have said anything further from the truth. "Not even a little bit."

As she studied his demeanor, she realized that she'd gotten more than she'd expected when she invited Cain to join her and Amy. A lot more. He was a pillar of strength. A worldly man with worldly views and a unique perspective, unlike any man she'd ever met.

He was the epitome of confidence, strength, and compassion. The last tree standing after a hurricane. The hand that grabbed your wrist as you fell over the edge of a cliff toward certain death. Cain was the person who pulled you back to safety and tended to your wounds with caring hands.

"Talking to you is just a lot easier than I thought it would be," she said.

He humbly lowered his chin. "I try to be a good listener."

"You're very good at it."

"It's a lost art these days."

"Yes, it is." People nowadays seemed too busy burying their noses in their phones and monitoring how many likes their latest post got. They didn't actually pay attention to their surroundings or listen to the people in their lives. Even now, half the people at the party had their phones out, taking selfies, checking social media, shooting videos of the DJ and others at the party.

Cain hadn't checked his phone once. Did he even have one on him?

"So, anyway," she continued, trying to focus on anything other than how hard he made her heart beat. "After the accident, I quit school to take care of Kai, and my agoraphobia returned like a bad rash that never quite heals, going from manageable to out of control on a dime." She snapped her fingers. "The world went back to being this big, scary place, and I went back to being a prisoner in my own home most of the time." She ended with a resigned shrug. "Is that pathetic or what?"

His brow dipped, pinching over the bridge of his nose. "Not at all. You're not pathetic for being human, Rayna. You're just a little broken right now, that's all." He squeezed her hand and gave her a reassuring smile. "And being a little broken isn't a bad thing. It proves you've been an active participant in life. We're born perfect, but life adds imperfection. Life gets hold of us and adds scars to our souls. Some of those scars are deeper than others, and some take longer to heal, but it's those scars that give you character." His gaze circled her face. "It's those scars that make you beautiful."

For a long moment, all she could do was stare back at him. Her heart had been beating hard before, but now it pounded like Thor's hammer against her rib cage.

Who was this man? Where had he come from? And could she bottle him and take him out any time she needed a dose of courage or a compliment that made her toes curl? Because Cain had a way with words that touched her in ways she'd never experienced.

"Then you must have a lot of scars," she said quietly, unable to tear her gaze from his sky-blue eyes.

It was a bold thing to say, especially for her. She'd never been good at flirting, never been the type to make the first move on a guy. Yet here she was, telling Cain in her own subtly bold manner that she thought he was beautiful too.

A slow grin spread over his mouth. "I do have a lot of scars."

And in that moment, she knew. He was the reason she'd come to this party. He was why she'd insisted on not going home. Because if she had, she wouldn't have met him, and they'd been destined to meet.

Cain had mended something inside her. One of her broken pieces. He'd glued it back into place. Adding to her scars. Scars that, according to him, made her beautiful.

CHAPTER FIVE

If you do not change direction, you may end up where you are heading.
—Lao Tzu

Twenty minutes ago, Cain never would have guessed Rayna's past could be so riddled with tragedy.

He could only imagine the pain and suffering she had endured.

Why did it have to happen to the good ones? Why couldn't death just take the bad ones? Like his parents? Specifically his father?

If he got the call tomorrow that his father had

died, he'd probably say something along the lines of "Good. It's about time that bastard got what he deserved." But he wouldn't have *felt* anything. No joy, no remorse. Just . . . void.

No doubt Baron Savage would live to be a hundred years old, just so he could maximize the amount of torture and pain he could inflict on the world.

Losing his mom would be a little different, but he doubted he would mourn her death either. If anything, he would mourn that she'd never allowed herself to *live*. He would be glad she no longer had to put up with his father. She wouldn't have to wear fake smiles in public anymore to make it appear that nothing was wrong, while within the walls of the family home she walked around like an apathetic ghost. She had never actually been a mother to him, instead pouring all her energy into creating the facade that all was well and shielding herself from his father.

Cain's parents could be the poster children for how to create a dysfunctional homelife. How he had turned out as a relatively decent guy with a heart was a testament to the influence Storm's parents had had on him, as well as the contractor who had taken him under his wing during the year he'd "taken off" after high school.

Taken off. Right. That's what he had wanted his prick of a father to think, but Cain's plan all along had been to get out of New York. The year apprenticing secretly with Roy had been the means to do that.

It was plain to see that Rayna's parents weren't like his own. She remembered them with fondness and mourned their deaths deep within her heart. Which meant they'd been good people. Because no one mourned the bad ones. Rayna's parents had probably been humanitarians who got involved with every philanthropic activity they could while never missing an after-school soccer game or choir recital.

Which made Rayna even more of a treasure. She was a Pandora's box. A fascination he was driven to explore. A rosebud he wanted to help open.

The music changed to something slower. Not a love song, but not the wild and up-tempo EDM the DJ had been playing thus far.

"Dance with me," he said, scooting to the edge of his seat.

Her eyes dropped to his mouth, and he could swear she was about to kiss him. Then she blinked like she'd just awakened from a trance, rearing back. "W-what?"

Either she hadn't heard him the first time, or she

had an aversion to dancing. An aversion most likely pronounced by her agoraphobia.

Well, it looked like she was just going to have to face her fear, because he wasn't taking no for an answer. If he didn't get Rayna in his arms one way or another in the next sixty seconds, he was going to lose his mind.

One second, Rayna had been fantasizing about taking the bull by the horns and kissing him, ready to follow him anywhere he wanted to take her. The next, he was pulling her hand forward and motioning to stand.

What had he said?

Dance with me.

Okay, so maybe she wouldn't follow him *anywhere*. There were limits. Dancing was one of them.

"W-what?" she said, recoiling like he'd asked her to go parachuting . . . without a parachute.

His hand tightened around hers. "Come on, dance with me," he said again, smiling disarmingly.

"I . . . I don't dance."

Chewing on her bottom lip, she stared past his shoulder at the mass of bodies swaying and moving in sensually slow gyrations on the dance floor. She'd always felt like she had two left feet when it came to finding a rhythm, but she'd never really danced with a man before. She and Shaun had never had time between her classes and his job to do much more than go out to dinner and park on his couch with a bowl of popcorn and a movie. And in high school, she'd been pinned too deeply inside agoraphobia's grasp to get out much to do anything at all, let alone go to school dances.

"Come on," he said, giving her arm a gentle tug. "Live a little."

Live a little.

Live a little.

LIVE.

Something snapped into place inside her.

When Amy had suggested earlier that they skip the party and go back to her house, Rayna had insisted on seeing this through. Why? Because she was tired of being afraid and of missing out on life. Because, in spite of her fears, she wanted to attend the party and not feel like she was a big fucking coward anymore, which was how she felt most of the time.

And wasn't that the reason why she had forced herself to stand on her own when Amy went to get them drinks before Cain showed up? Because she had wanted to prove she could do it? Because, ultimately, she had wanted to *live?* To choose living a full life over living in fear, which isn't living at all?

She stared into Cain's eyes. He was an immovable rock. Sturdy and reliable. Exactly what she needed to feel safe while dipping not just her toe, but also her whole damn leg into fear's chilly waters.

Taking a deep breath, she planted her stiletto'd feet on the floor and pushed off her chair with a nervous nod. "Okay."

He seemed to know instinctively not to make a big deal out of her acquiescence, smiling warmly and enveloping her hand completely with his as he led her toward the dance floor, guiding her with ease around the maze of tables, cushioned seats, and gathered clumps of people.

But it wasn't the only maze he was leading her through. With each step, she felt like he was guiding her out of the labyrinth of fear inside her head. The one she'd gotten lost in years ago. And the dance floor was the way out. If she could just make it there, she would be free.

As they neared the pulsating throng in the center of the room, her steps slowed. Not out of fear, but out of anticipation . . . and maybe a little reverence. This felt much bigger than it looked. Like she was about to complete a rite of passage she hadn't even known she'd undertaken.

It was crazy how such a simple thing could mean so much. She wasn't approaching the summit of Mount Kilimanjaro, or about to take gold in the Olympics like her brother had aspired to, or even saving a life—not in the literal sense, anyway. But she *could* argue that she was saving *her* life. The feeling of accomplishment was the same.

The moment she crossed the invisible boundary onto the dance floor, she released a breath she hadn't even realized she'd been holding. *Whoosh!* The air blasted from her lungs. A second later, she started laughing.

Cain leaned down and spoke loudly enough to be heard over the music as the throng swallowed them. "What's so funny?" His expression was both amused and curious.

With a shake of her head, she latched onto his forearm with her free hand as dancing bodies pressed in, jostling her, pushing her closer to him. "Nothing, it's just . . ." She couldn't find the word.

He faced her. "Stimulating?" His arm wound around her waist and tugged her forward.

She drew in her breath and nodded, abruptly dazed as the front of her body met his.

Stimulating was the perfect word for how she was

being affected, not just by the music, the other dancers, and having made it to the promised land, but by him. His proximity. His scent. The way his mesmerizing blue eyes drank in her face.

He smelled delicious. Felt even better. Warm, solid, firm in all the right places. Her hand skimmed up his biceps to his shoulder, then down to his chest. As she explored, his muscles twitched beneath her palm, almost as if he enjoyed her touching him as much as she did.

It had been a long time since she'd touched a man like this. She didn't remember it ever feeling this way, though. Like she was touching a *real man*. A man not trying to hide his most feral qualities behind a veneer of false propriety.

I like sex. That's what he'd said. *I think about. I've thought about it with you.*

Was he thinking about it now? With his stormy eyes locked to hers, and their bodies swaying to a sultry, deep-bass beat, was he imagining how her naked body would feel pressed against his?

She stepped closer, purposely pressing her breasts against his chest. She was testing him for a reaction. Tempting him. Seducing him. She hadn't intended to. It just happened. Her body took over, and her mind blindly followed. No hesitation. No voice of caution boomed inside her head, warning her to stop. So she didn't.

Emboldened, she let go of his hand and used both of hers to feel the man beneath the clothes. The hard curves of his biceps, the solid arch of his shoulders, the firm swell of his chest, which expanded on a deep inhale as the corners of his mouth curled in a knowing grin.

She smiled back, letting her gaze drop to his mouth. God, she wanted to kiss him. The compulsion to do so barely left room for her nervous system to perform simple tasks such as breathing and blinking.

Maybe this was what happened when you were faced with a man hotter than Adonis after not having so much as a date for five years. Or maybe she was just riding the high of making it to the dance floor without folding in on herself like a turtle ducking into its shell. Both?

Whatever the reason, she couldn't get the thought of him fucking her out of her brain. Against a wall, on the floor, in a chair, on the bed, in the shower. The flashing images felt like premonitions of what was going to happen between them, not fantasies about what she *wanted* to happen. Not mere daydreams she could masturbate to in the privacy of her bedroom later, but the real thing.

The most amazing part about all this was how much she'd transformed since she'd arrived at the party less than an hour ago. Hell, she'd barely been able to get out of the Uber and walk in the door. Less than forty minutes ago, she'd been talking herself down from the ledge where fear and sanity met. Now she was contemplating locking lips with a man she barely knew and wondering if he was as good in bed as he was with words, because just his words had sparked a fire low in her belly that still smoldered, waiting for a shot of kerosene to completely consume her.

Most importantly, she wasn't looking at him and seeing all the potentially awful things he could do to her and all the horrible ways spending the night with him could end. For the first time in a long while, she was excited. Not just sexually excited, but excited about life. About living, exploring, taking risks, and trying something new. She hadn't felt this way since before she left for college.

He was hope. Hope for the future, for change . . . for *recovery*. She looked at him and saw a reason to heal. A reason not to give up. To keep fighting to get her life back.

Did that mean he was her future husband? No. She didn't get that vibe at all. But was he somebody meaningful? Yes. Somebody pivotal to her personal growth? Most certainly. And was tonight a night she might be able to look back on five years from now and say, "That's when I turned a corner, that's when I began to get my life back"? Definitely.

Something cathartic had unlocked inside her in the last five minutes. A purge. A cleansing of her soul. She'd felt it with her first step onto the dance floor. A warmth had vibrated to life inside her chest and spread throughout her whole body, all the way to the tips of her fingers and toes.

I crossed the room to meet you, not because you're the most beautiful woman here—which you are—but because you are the only woman at this party who looks like she has something to say that I actually want to hear.

He hadn't been lying when he told her that. That hadn't been just some lame line he'd used to get his hands up her skirt. He'd genuinely meant it. He was honestly more interested in what she possessed between her ears than what lay between her legs.

This was a man who knew how to make love to a woman's mind as well as her body, whether it was for one night, one year, or a lifetime. And right now, despite every reason the last eleven years had given her to think otherwise, it was what lay between her legs she wanted him focusing on.

"I know it sounds cliché," he said, speaking loudly enough to be heard over the music without yelling, "but given the look on your face right now, as well as the way you're touching me, I'm dying to know what you're thinking."

Warmth rushed into her cheeks as she dropped her gaze to where her fingers splayed over his blue shirt, the heat of his body pouring into her palms. "I don't know . . ." *Liar, liar, liar.* She so knew what she was thinking, and it included a collection of some of the dirtiest, naughtiest, and most salacious thoughts she'd ever conjured.

His shallow grin twisted into a knowing smirk, and he reached up to tuck a strand of hair behind her ear. "Oh, I think you do." His fingertips skimmed down her cheek to her chin.

"I . . ." Her gaze dropped to his mouth again.

What she wanted was for him to obliterate her reality. To rock her world with such ferocity that every wall she'd erected came crashing down in bits of rubble and dust, giving her no choice but to rebuild her existence from scratch.

But she couldn't say that to him. Could she?

"I . . ." She briefly closed her eyes, trying to make sense of what she was feeling even as her fantasies escalated and her pulse raced.

When she opened her eyes again, he was watching her with the kind of interest a lion shows an injured gazelle on feeding day. The burning desire in his expression was enough to make her suck in her breath and blurt, "What are *you* thinking?"

One eyebrow arched as if her question mildly amused him. "That's a loaded question, Rayna." The blue flames in his eyes burned brighter as he gazed at her mouth.

She bit her lip at the suggestive way he was looking at her, feeling tendrils of warmth unfurl in her belly. "Loaded? Why?"

He pressed closer, his eyes traveling around her face. "Because I'm thinking a lot of things. And I'm willing to bet most are the same things you're thinking."

I like sex. I've thought about it with you.

His hand slid farther around her waist to the small of her back, then down lower, over the upper swell of her bottom, where he gently but suggestively tightened his grip.

Heat erupted inside her core, expanding swiftly outward, making her suck in her breath.

She weaved forward, closing her eyes and tipping her forehead against his cheek. "I've never felt like this before."

He lightly cradled the back of her head. "I can't imagine why," he said lightheartedly. "It's not like you haven't been through hell for the past eleven years."

It sounded like such a long time and yet it didn't feel like it.

His fingers caressed the nape of her neck and down her shoulder. "You've been going through hell for eleven years, Rayna. I'm not surprised you've never felt this way." His fingertips trailed lightly down the back of her arm. "It feels good, doesn't it?"

She gulped past the cotton in her throat. "Yes."

She'd never met a bolder or more desirable man. A man who skillfully and blatantly avoided beating around the bush. A man who didn't hide behind fake smiles and false pretenses.

The irony of the situation wasn't lost on her. He hid from no one and nothing, while she hid from everyone and everything. Hell, she'd even given him a fake name. Talk about hiding. She was an expert.

His mouth was only inches from hers. All it would take to kiss him would be for her to lift her head, shift a little this way, turn a little that way, and she'd achieve another first.

She licked her lips. Could she be so bold? She had been once, a long time ago. That same fearless child still resided in her somewhere. Maybe finding her courageous inner twelve-year-old was the key to stomping her phobia into the past once and for all. But how exactly did she go about doing that?

He wound both arms around her waist, pulling

her even closer, causing her heart to skip a beat before kicking into high gear as her knees threatened to give. But not from fear. From *arousal*.

Holy shit, she was five-alarm turned on! No fear anywhere in sight. Only need. Powerful sexual desire.

Dragging his lips up to her ear, he invaded her personal space in a way no man had in over five years and whispered just loud enough for her to hear over the music, "You excite me. Everything about you excites me." His lips brushed her earlobe, eliciting a shiver down her back that spread into her arms and legs.

"You excite me too," she replied, feeling like her feet were no longer touching the floor.

The tips of his fingers glided down her spine, along the zipper of her dress, making her shiver.

"Are you scared?" he asked.

That was just it, she wasn't. Not in the least. She was shaking because something monumental was happening inside her body, and she was having a hard time keeping whatever it was contained.

She shook her head.

"You're not?" He sounded surprised. "Then why are you trembling?"

"Because . . ." She closed her eyes, beginning to lose her restraint. How could a thin layer of skin hold back this much sexual response without disintegrating in a fiery explosion?

He bowed his head beside hers. "How long has it been?" He kept his voice soft, quiet, gently prying away her walls.

She knew exactly what he was asking without him saying more.

"Too long," she murmured, certain he hadn't heard her over the loud music.

"One year? Two?" he probed.

She shook her head.

"Three?"

She bit her lip and raised her chin, feeling the rough scratch of his beard on her cheek. She sighed, letting her face slide against his, enjoying the manly abrasion. How would his beard feel on her inner thighs? Between her legs?

"Four?" he asked, winding his arm almost all the way around her waist and tugging her so tightly against him she felt like their bodies were fusing into one. "Five?"

She pulled back just enough that she could look him in the eye.

He must have seen in her expression the confirmation he sought, because his face softened. "Five." The single syllable sounded like the end of the discussion. "Five years."

She nodded. It was close enough, give or take a couple of months. That was the last time she'd been touched by a man's hands. The last time she'd felt the fire of pleasure inside her. The last time she'd been kissed.

She didn't want to wait any longer.

Before she was even fully aware of what she was doing, her mouth snapped to his like they were a pair of magnets.

He seemed surprised, unprepared for such a swift assault. But he recovered quickly, exhaling on a moan as his lips parted with hers, his tongue sweeping over hers in a possessive blaze that felt like victory.

The kiss was everything she'd imagined it would be and more. Both fire and ice. Rough and gentle. Stormy and calm. On the verge of wild abandon yet fully controlled.

It seemed she'd found the way back to her inner badass. Jump. Leap. Not just step off the cliff, but run off of it before she had a chance to think too much about what she was doing.

She was running.

She was jumping.

She was falling.

And for the first time in years, she didn't care where or how hard she landed.

CHAPTER SIX

The only way to make sense out of change is to plunge into it, move with it, and join the dance.
—Alan Watts

Cain hadn't expected her to kiss him. Hadn't expected her to launch into him and claim his lips like a starving woman devouring her first meal in weeks.

But wasn't that what she was? Starving?

Five years.

Rayna hadn't been touched in five years. Not like this. Not in the most intimate way a man could touch a woman.

But based on the way she was kissing him, she'd chosen him to remedy the situation. To end the celibacy years of fear had forced on her.

She'd chosen him as much as he'd chosen her, and he wouldn't let her down. If she wanted a night with him, he would willingly give it and make it as good as she deserved.

But if he didn't slow things down, he was going to blow his whole speech about being the kind of man who could control himself. Because he was two heartbeats away from throwing her over his shoulder and cavemanning her up to his room.

He forced himself to pull away, breaking the kind of kiss that said "fuck me now" in every language.

The moment their lips separated, all he wanted was to kiss her again. "Maybe we should go sit down," he said, barely managing to restrain himself.

Sitting would be good. That kiss had gotten him so hard it was a miracle he hadn't split the seam of his pants.

Her gaze remained locked on his mouth, her brown eyes blazing in a way that left no question about how she was feeling or what she wanted. No doubt she was seeing the same look in his own eyes, because he wanted her in a way he hadn't wanted a woman in a long time. There was something electric between them, a craving he hadn't felt in years.

It looked like tonight was heading in a very clear direction, which would allow them to know each other a whole lot better by morning, but that didn't mean they had to rush. And if she was going to spend the night with him, he wanted her to make that decision with a clear head. The last thing he wanted was for her to wake up in the morning, take one look at him, and think "Oh my God, what have I done?" before running back to the hiding place she appeared to have extracted herself from.

No guilt. No regrets. That was the only way this would work.

"Come on." He brushed his lips over her forehead, then took her hand and nudged her toward the periphery of the mass of swaying bodies.

She appeared as dazed as he felt, as swept away on lust as he was.

He could only imagine the damage they could do to each other. Or the treat he and Storm could have given her together.

There was no question Storm would have liked her. She was just his type, a little wounded but with enough fight to make her a wild card. And, like Cain, Storm had a thing for women with dark hair. No doubt he would have chosen Rayna from the crowd, too, if he'd attended the party.

It wouldn't have been the first time he and Storm

had picked the same woman out of a crowd. Not even the second. They both tended to gravitate to the same women, only from different angles. While Storm enjoyed the way wounded women with lady balls kept him guessing and never gave him a dull day, Cain enjoyed feeling like the savior who could heal their damaged hearts . . . and maybe tame them a little in the process.

For open-minded women who didn't mind being shared, it presented an opportunity for everyone to be happy. Something he and Storm had discovered after nearly ending their friendship ten years ago after a woman Storm had been seeing—but said he wasn't serious about—ended up in Cain's bed.

Apparently, Storm had been more serious about her than he'd let on. He'd been so upset they'd almost parted ways. Instead, they made a pact never to fight over a woman again. They'd since had more than a few three-way relationships with women who didn't mind being the cream filling in their cookie.

Of course, not every woman was down with sharing, but those who were never disappointed.

Rayna wouldn't have been disappointed either. He had a feeling he and Storm were just what she needed.

But Storm wasn't there.

Rayna was all his for the night if she would have him.

He grabbed them a couple of drinks, then led her back to their table in the corner on the lower level.

Taking her hand, he pulled her against him as they sat, not wanting her any farther away than was necessary. Settling in beside her, he wrapped his arm around her shoulders. After that kiss, he was entitled to let the other men in the room know she was with him and that any man who tried to horn in would meet with difficulties.

The way she scooted closer and rested her hand on the inner curve of his thigh, she wanted to send the same message to the other women.

Not that she needed to worry. He already had what he wanted. No other woman at the party even compared to her.

Rayna was too shocked to speak. Shocked by the cauldron of butterflies in her stomach, the repeating loop of torrid thoughts cycling through her mind, the slick arousal between her legs, and most of all, her own audacity to take the reins and kiss him like she was ready to fuck him.

She lifted her fingertips to her mouth, feeling the

swollen warmth of her lips, amazed her skin wasn't actually on fire right now. It should have been, because her insides were a river of flowing lava.

"I can't believe . . ." She bit her bottom lip and glanced furtively at him.

"What?" he asked. "What can't you believe?"

It was as if they were the only two people there. The other guests, the music, the DJ, it all disappeared the moment her eyes met his.

"I kissed you," she said quietly.

Blue heat flared in his eyes as they dropped to her mouth. "Yes, you did."

"You must think I'm—"

"Fucking incredible," he finished, driving the fingers of his free hand up her cheek and into her hair as he bent toward her and claimed her mouth with his.

Every nerve in her body lit up like he'd doused her in gasoline and struck a match.

She'd never been kissed like that. Her last boyfriend hadn't even come *close* to kissing her that way. So primal. So feral. Plundering her like a Viking horde conquering new territory.

Too long, it's been too long.

She knew her powerful response was fueled by five years of celibacy, but that wasn't the only reason. Cain had skills. Skills other men didn't. At least no man she'd ever dated, which wasn't many. But she'd kissed guys before. She'd had sex. But never like this. Hell, her clothes were still on, but she was already on the verge of coming. Just from his mouth on hers and the way his hand gripped her cheek as if he were forcing himself not to touch her elsewhere.

She *wanted* him to touch her elsewhere. She wanted that hand on her bare skin, her breasts, her thighs, between her legs. Everywhere.

She broke the kiss but didn't pull away. "Take me to your room," she said breathlessly against his mouth.

Her therapist always reminded her to live in the moment, but until right now, she hadn't fully understood what that meant. Now she did, because for once, she was squarely inside the moment, not thinking about the past or the future, but focused squarely on now.

His fingers curled against her face. "But—"

"No." Her own fingers were already knotted around a ball of light-blue fabric along the placket of his shirt. "Don't give me time to think about it. Just take me."

She tightened her grip, lifting her eyes to his, beseeching him. She knew she was begging. Knew she was shattering every code of safe behavior and abandoning logic and caution, embracing risk, exposing herself to danger. But she didn't care. She didn't want safe. She wanted him. She wanted *this*. *Needed* it in a way she couldn't put into words. She just knew it was the key to unlocking herself from her self-made prison.

Years of playing it safe had gotten her exactly nowhere. She was still the terrified little girl she'd been after her mother disappeared eleven years ago. When was she going to grow up? Grow out of this illogical dread that pending doom awaited her around every corner?

What she needed was to face her fear head-on. To not only look it in the eye but wrestle it down by the horns and stomp its head in the dirt.

This is my *life, bitch!*

When Cain didn't immediately respond and only stared back at her like he was caught inside his own internal battle of whether he should deny her or surrender, she released his shirt and dropped her hand to his crotch. He was hard. Iron hard.

He jerked, then groaned, his gaze turning glassy as her fingers curled around his erection.

"Please," she said, her lips brushing over his. "Take me back to your room."

She didn't need to voice what she wanted him to do to her once he got her there. The way her hand massaged the steely length inside his pants told him everything he needed to know.

Closing his eyes, he tipped his forehead against hers and moaned, caressing her cheek with his thumb. "Are you sure this is what you want?"

She stroked him through his pants again. "Yes."

She didn't even know his last name, but it didn't matter. The less she knew about him the better. This was about facing her fears, not softening the blow with facts and details.

His palm trailed down her arm, sending goose bumps all over her body. "Tell your friend first. Text her." He leaned back and bobbed his head toward her handbag, where her phone was. "Tell her where you're going. Now."

He didn't have to tell her twice. She quickly fished out her phone and typed out a quick text to Amy.

RAYNA: *I'm going to Cain's room. Don't try to stop me. I'm fine. I'm safe. I need this. I'll call you in the morning. Happy New Year! Love you.*

Without waiting for a reply, she dropped her phone into her bag and snapped it shut. "Let's go." She was shaking. From adrenaline? Fear? Excitement? All of the above?

He downed the last swallow of his drink, clunked his empty glass on the table, and took her hand as he stood.

Lacing her fingers around his and hanging on tight, she let him lead her out of Skybar, into the hotel, and into an elevator, where he practically punched the button for his floor.

He was breathing hard. So was she. Sexual tension nearly strangled her as warmth pulsed between her legs, making her shift from side to side, seeking relief as they waited for the doors to close.

"Uncomfortable?" he asked quietly, his voice low and strained.

"No."

He raised one eyebrow and looked down at her.

She bit her lip and squirmed at the slippery sensation between her legs.

The corners of his mouth suddenly quirked upward as if he'd figured out why she was so twitchy.

Facing front again as the doors began to slide shut, he asked, "How wet are you?"

She swayed toward him, clutching his arm as her knees trembled. "V-very."

He made a quiet, choked sound deep inside his throat, his muscles clenching beneath her hands.

The moment the doors sealed shut he turned sharply and shoved her back against the wall, slamming her hand on the polished wood beside her head, his mouth crashing down over hers in a furious storm, like a strike of lightning scorching her senses. His other hand yanked up the skirt of her dress and clamped down over the heat between her legs.

She almost came, gasping into his mouth as her thighs clinched together, holding his hand in place.

"Yes. Rough," she said. "Be rough with me. Rough is good. Don't be gentle."

She didn't need gentle. Gentle would give her time to think. Time to get too far inside her head. Time to reconsider what she was doing and back out. She couldn't have that. Just like coming to the party, she needed to see this through, so the rougher the better. Hard, brutal, bruising. That was the key to distracting her mind enough to make this work.

"Fuck." He growled against her mouth. "Who are you, and where did you hide Rayna?"

She fisted the hair on the back of his head, holding him where she wanted him. "Fuck Rayna."

He chuckled and nipped her top lip with his teeth as he pushed aside her panties and slicked his fingers up and down her center, making her nearly pass out. "Oh, I plan to." His pupils dilated and the tip of his tongue wet his lips as his fingers slid forward and back. "Mmm, you *are* wet."

The elevator dinged, and he pulled away like he was a man on a mission, snatching her hand in his, practically dragging her out of the elevator before the doors were fully open. Walking with purpose and holding his fingers under his nose as he inhaled her scent with a lusty, possessive growl, he led her down the hall. About halfway down, he stopped in front of his room, whipped his key card from his pocket, and swiped it through the lock.

A moment later, the door closed behind her as she stepped inside. The room was dark and well appointed, not that she had much time to notice. In an instant, he had her back pressed against the wall beside the door, his hands up her skirt, thumbs hooking the elastic waist of her panties. In a flash, he pushed them down her legs, kneeling in front of her.

"Open your legs," he commanded, placing his hands on the inside of her knees and pushing.

"What are you do—?"

"Open them."

Without thinking, she did as he demanded.

His palms drove up her inner thighs. "Lift your dress."

"But—"

"You said you didn't want to think, so don't. Just do it."

God, yes! He instinctively knew what she needed and was willingly playing along.

"You want it rough?" he said with a snarl. "I'll give you rough."

Shuddering from the wave of exhilaration and anticipation that shot through her, she dropped her handbag on the floor and clutched the metallic fabric of her dress with trembling hands.

Don't think. Do it.

Taking a shaky breath, she lifted her skirt, exposing herself. She refused to close her eyes. She needed to witness his response the moment he saw her naked flesh.

His nostrils flared and his eyes sharpened, every part of him focused on what she'd just revealed.

"Fuck." His gaze flicked to hers only briefly before dropping hungrily back to her core.

"Please . . ." She squirmed against his hold on her thighs.

He was taking too much time, letting her thoughts catch up to her.

Sensing her desperation, he licked his lips, smirked, then nearly toppled her over as his hands contracted around her inner thighs and opened her even wider, his thumbs parting her lips a split second before he plunged forward and clamped his mouth on her clit.

Her vision went dark as she threw back her head and cried out. His tongue lashed, his mouth drew her in, sucking and teasing. Within seconds, she was shaking so violently her teeth chattered, her hips grinding against his face.

Before she even knew what was happening, she was coming. Coming harder than she ever had. She was still coming as he rose in front of her and spun her around.

"You come like an angel." He spoke softly into her hair, his voice a low rumble.

Slapping her hands against the wall, she shuddered through another series of contractions as he took the zipper tab on her dress and zinged it down her back.

"Drop your arms," he said sternly.

She did, and the dress fell into a puddle of metallic fabric on the floor as her legs shuddered and nearly gave out. Less than two seconds later, her bra joined her dress. Except for her shoes, she was totally naked.

"Is this good?" he whispered hotly, pressing himself against her from behind, wrapping his arms around her hips, pulling her back to feel his erection against her bottom.

She nodded, unable to speak.

"You want more?"

Another nod, more urgent this time. She could already feel another orgasm queuing up.

"Rough?"

Nod.

"You like it rough?"

This time, she found her voice. "Y-yes." Rough was good. Rough was cleansing.

He yanked her away from the wall so sharply that she yelped, then he spun her toward the bed.

Arousal spiked again as he shoved her onto the edge of the mattress and began unfastening the buttons on his shirt at record speed. "So this is Renita?" he said with a sexy smirk.

She nodded and reached for his belt, feeling the alter ego she'd made up an hour ago take over. Even though she was shaking from the adrenaline pouring into her blood, she made quick work unfastening the belt and pulling it free of the loops. As he released the snap and zipper on his trousers and let them fall to his ankles, she stared at the belt. It was made of soft black leather with a brushed silver buckle.

She was still holding it as he pushed her back on the bed and reached for the drawer on the nightstand.

"Tie me up," she murmured, her fingers tightening around the leather.

He froze, a strip of condoms in his hand. "What?"

She was almost panting as she lifted the belt. "Tie me up," she said more boldly. "Bind my hands."

He frowned as if he wasn't sure that was such a good idea. "Are you sure?"

No.

"Yes." She shoved the belt at him before she could change her mind. It was tempting to ask him to blindfold her, too, but that might have been taking things too far. Besides, she liked seeing the expression on his face as his desire ratcheted up with hers. It made her feel powerful.

He tore off one of the condoms, tossed the square packet onto the bed, then took the belt and straddled her torso. He still wore his boxers, but they rode low on his hips as if he'd begun to push them down, which allowed the head of his erection to peek out from the waistband.

It was thick, swollen, and ruddy. In only a few short moments, it would be inside her. Her breath came in short bursts at the thought.

Lifting her arms, she pressed her wrists together. Part of her couldn't believe she was doing this. The other part was about to leap out of her skin with anticipation as he began wrapping the strap of leather around her wrists.

Fear threatened as he tugged the looped leather tight, securing the buckle. She was fully bound. Her chest began to constrict.

"Fuck me." She gasped, throwing her restrained hands over her head on the pillow and opening her legs. "Fuck me *now*."

He was already one step ahead of her, shedding his boxers as if he sensed the urgency of the moment and the small window of time he had to subdue her panic. His erection sprang forward, bobbing as he kicked his boxers off his feet and ripped open the packet.

"Hurry." She writhed, pulling against the belt, unable to break free, watching him roll on the latex sheath. "Hurry!"

Spreading her thighs, he slicked the head of his cock up and down her opening, positioning himself. Then he planted his palms on the backs of her bent knees, holding her legs open wide, and plunged into her with a satisfied grunt.

She cried out, her upper body arching off the bed before crashing back into the mattress as he began pumping into her at a breakneck pace.

"Yes! Harder!"

He gave her what she demanded, pounding into

her with enough force to push her up the comforter toward the headboard, their bodies slapping together.

Releasing one leg, he clutched her breast, squeezing painfully.

"YES! More!"

Within seconds, his body was glistening with sweat, the muscles in his chest and shoulders drawn tight, his abdomen working hard over washboard ridges.

"You want more?" he barked in choppy syllables.

She nodded, her fingers stretching against her restraints, her free leg wrapping around his back.

A dark sneer flashed over his face. A moment later, he pulled out of her, grabbed her ankles, and flipped her onto her stomach. Her face planted against the soft comforter, and she turned her head and pushed up onto her elbows.

In a blink, he covered her back, urging her hips off the bed, impaling her again in one swift stroke.

Her eyes flew open wide as she shot forward. Holy shit! What was he doing to her? She'd never felt anything like this before. Never been taken from behind. But, omigod! Stars shot through her vision.

Strong, rough hands gripped her hips, holding her in place as he thrust into her like his own survival depended on it.

Without warning, her insides tightened, radiating molten fire into her stomach.

"I'm going to come!" She didn't even sound like herself, wanton, frenzied, frantic. "Don't stop, God please don't stop!"

As she released more violently than before, he exhaled a long, intensifying groan, pumping furiously, the front of his hips slapping loudly against her ass.

"Fuck," he bit out. "Fuck!" His hips plowed forward, propelling her toward the headboard.

Her elbows gave, and she fell face-first onto the mattress as he shuddered and convulsed through his own release, collapsing over her back as his hips continuing pulsing into her.

She no longer cared that her hands were bound. No longer cared that she didn't know his last name, didn't know anything about him other than the barest details, and had only just met him a little over an hour ago.

What did matter was, for the first time in years, she was living solidly in the moment. There was no scary past. There was no unknown future. There was only now. Right now. On this bed. Her body singing. His warmth pressed against her.

Purged.

With Cain, she'd achieved catharsis.

Her fear was nowhere to be found.

CHAPTER SEVEN

Flow with whatever may happen and let your mind be free.
—Chuang Tzu

It was almost midnight. Only seconds left.

Rayna heard the crowd below at Skybar counting down. It was almost a new year. A new beginning.

Rayna held Cain's body against hers.

"You're close?" he asked softly, his voice tight, shallowly pumping in and out of her, already on the verge of letting go.

"Yes," she whispered, digging her fingers into his

back. His muscles bunched and flexed against her palms.

"Together," he whispered before brushing his lips over the side of her neck in a hot caress. "We come together."

She nodded, nipping his shoulder, letting her teeth remain against his skin. How many times had she come tonight? Four? Five? It hadn't been enough.

"Ten, nine, eight . . ." the crowd below chanted.

Cain had opened the sliding glass door to his balcony thirty minutes ago, inviting the party into his room, before climbing back into bed beside her and working her up for one last go before the clock struck twelve.

His strokes grew longer, more pronounced, punctuated with a forward thrust that forced his pubic bone to collide with her clit.

". . .six, five, four . . ."

She dug her teeth into Cain's shoulder and squeezed her eyes closed. She wasn't sure she could hold out for four more seconds. From the urgent grunts squeezing from his throat, it didn't sound like Cain was going to be able to either.

". . . two, one . . ."

As the crowd broke into cheers of "HAPPY NEW YEAR!" and fireworks boomed and exploded off the top of the hotel, creating flashes of red-and-white light outside, Cain's body seized with hers.

Violent trembles ranged through her body, and she locked her arms around him, legs quivering, as he let go inside her, jerking and kicking against her inner walls.

Lifting his head from beside hers, he kissed her. It was sweet and breathless and sincere.

"Happy New Year," he said, letting his nose bump playfully against hers.

She smiled against his mouth. "Happy New Year."

CHAPTER EIGHT

*Twenty years from now you will be more disappointed by
the things you didn't do than by the ones you did do.*
—Mark Twain

All was quiet. The party had long since ended. The DJ had packed up hours ago, the guests departing for home or other—more private—parties.

The new year was already five hours old.

Rayna sat in the chair beside the bed in her wrinkled dress, her hair a sex-disheveled mess, watching Cain sleep. What little makeup she'd been wearing had long been rubbed off on Cain's body, the sheets, or the pillowcases.

He looked so peaceful, so calm, not like the Cain who had ravished her only hours before.

She'd been tempted to fish his wallet from his pants pocket to sneak a peek at his ID, but she had decided against it. She didn't want to ruin what they'd shared, and learning his last name would do just that. Because then she'd be tempted to look him up, track him down on Facebook or Instagram, to follow him through his worldly travels. And that would just make her sad . . . and maybe a little pathetic.

No, it was better she didn't know any details about him. They'd had one night. One incredible night fueled by her need to conquer her fear. And she had. She'd slept with a stranger. She'd put herself squarely in the center of everything that would have emotionally, mentally, and physically destroyed her a week ago, and she'd survived.

She grinned down at the coiled black leather belt clutched in her hand. A souvenir. A reminder. A talisman that, every time she looked at it from this day forward, would remind her of her strength and courage. That she didn't have to be afraid anymore. That, more or less, she was cured.

She could feel it in her soul. It might take time

for the rest of her body to accept what her brain already had, but last night had changed her. Changed her in ways she couldn't yet comprehend. But she could feel the essence of a new beginning unfurling in her heart. A new beginning Cain had helped her find. He'd been the catalyst. The impetus that had forced her to face the scary monster inside her head. He was the reason she felt like a shiny diamond carved from the rough.

She checked her phone. Her Uber would be out front in less than two minutes.

Amy had texted her too.

AMY: *Have fun and tell me all about it tomorrow. You deserve this.*

With a sad smile, she gave Cain a wistful glance, doing the best she could in those last few seconds to memorize the lines of his face and everything about him.

She could have taken a picture, but that would have violated her need to keep things distant. It also would have risked waking him. And if he woke before she could sneak out the door, she would stay, and she couldn't stay, because staying would destroy the magic of what they'd shared.

She had to leave. Now.

With the note she'd written him on hotel letterhead in her hand, she quietly stood, tiptoed to the dresser, and placed it near his shaving kit.

She glanced down at the belt in her hand. Was it fair that she was taking something of his without leaving something of hers? After considering it for a moment, she set down her handbag, quickly shimmied out of her panties, and dropped them by the note. It was proof of just how far she'd come in less than twelve hours, because the thought of going out in public in a dress like this without panties on would have been unthinkable to her twenty-four hours ago. Now she possessed the confidence to do exactly that without so much as a thought.

With one last glance over her shoulder at the man who'd changed her life, accomplishing in only a few hours what years and hundreds of hours of therapy had never been able to, she slipped out of the room as quietly as a thief.

She rode down to the lobby in the same elevator she and Cain had been in last night. She stared at the wall where he'd held her and ravaged her mouth, lighting a fire that still, deep inside her, smoldered.

She had a feeling it would be days if not weeks before the fire he'd started completely flickered out.

Closing her eyes so she could better relive the memories of all they'd done to each other, she sighed and let herself get lost for a few seconds. Was she making a mistake by sneaking away? Should she go back? Slide back into bed beside him? See where the day took them?

Oh, the temptation.

She opened her eyes and looked down at the floor. Leaving was the right choice. There was no future with Cain, and she shouldn't pretend there would be. In a few days, he would be gone. That's what he'd said last night. He was going to Portland.

Last night would have to be enough.

She stepped outside just as her Uber pulled to the curb. The sidewalk was littered with glittery streamers and empty cups, but the street was all but empty, which was a miracle for Los Angeles.

"Happy New Year," the driver said as she slipped into the back seat. He was far too chipper for this early in the morning.

"Happy New Year." She buckled her seat belt and looked back at the Mondrian with tears in her eyes as they began to pull away, her heart welling with both sadness and gratitude. She felt like she was leaving a tiny piece of herself behind, but taking something far greater away with her.

For as long as she lived, she would never forget last night. It would forever be the night when everything changed. When she'd found herself again.

"It's another new year," the driver said, sipping from a steaming Starbucks cup. "A new beginning."

She smiled out the window at the dark, early morning sky and city lights in the distance. It *was* a new beginning. And not just according to the calendar. She was starting over too.

"Did you make any resolutions?" the driver asked.

She had stopped making resolutions the year after her mom disappeared. She hadn't seen the point anymore. But now? She looked down at the black leather belt still clutched in her hand. Maybe she should start the tradition again.

"Ma'am?" the driver said.

She wiped away a rogue tear and smiled back at him in the rearview mirror. "Yes." Hope and anticipation bubbled up inside her, because, for the first time in over a decade, she looked forward to what lay ahead. "Yes, I did. I resolved to live fearlessly."

She sat a little taller, nodding more to herself than to the driver. *Here's to the year of living fearlessly.* She made a silent toast.

It wouldn't be easy, and she still had plenty of challenges to overcome, but last night showed her she had it in her to do just that. Now she just had to harness that knowledge and make it work for her. And she would. She could feel it.

And Cain had been the key to unlock her power.

CHAPTER NINE

In three words, I can sum up everything I've learned about life: it goes on.
—Robert Frost

Cain,

Thank you for last night. I'll never forget it, or you. You were exactly what I needed, exactly when I needed it. I have no regrets. I think I'll be okay now.

Happy New Year,

Rayna

P.S. I hope you don't mind, but I kept your belt as a souvenir.

Cain held Rayna's panties in one hand and her note in the other, not really sure how he felt about waking up to find her gone. He'd hoped to take her to breakfast. Maybe even dinner. To end up back here in his room tonight for more of what they'd shared last night.

But she'd taken all his plans with her when she left without even waking him to say goodbye.

He understood why she'd done it, but while he wasn't the sort to get attached, he had really hoped for a couple more days with her before he left to meet up with Storm in Portland.

His phone dinged.

Speak of the devil.

STORM: *How was last night? Meet anyone interesting?*

If only he knew.

CAIN: *Interesting is hardly the word I'd use.*

He grinned at the black satin panties in his hand. *Interesting* didn't even come close. Enigmatic.

Fascinating. Enchanting. Rayna was all those things and more.

STORM: *Is that good or bad?*

CAIN: *Very good. You would have liked her.*

STORM: *Then I'm sorry I missed it.*

CAIN: *Yeah. Me too. She needs the kind of paradigm shift you and I could have given her.*

STORM: *That sounds ominous.*

CAIN: *She's been through major shit. I'll tell you about it later.*

He didn't want to get into the story about what had happened to her parents in a text.

STORM: *Maybe I should return to LA. ;)*

CAIN: *Too late. She's already gone.*

STORM: *Gone? Did you kick her out?*

CAIN: *Fuck you.*

Storm knew he wasn't a dick like that. Before Storm could reply, Cain typed out a follow-up.

CAIN: *She was gone when I woke up.*

STORM: *Damn. That's cold.*

CAIN: *She had her reasons. But she left her panties, so it's all good.*

STORM: *She left them on purpose?*

Cain laughed out loud.

CAIN: *Yes, asshole. And she took my belt.*

STORM: *WTF? Why?*

Cain thought about the way she'd practically begged him to tie her up. The eager—almost desperate— look in her eyes as she held her joined wrists up for him to bind them. No wonder she'd wanted his belt as a souvenir.

CAIN: *Long story.*

STORM: *Tell me later. The doc just came in to check on Lora. Gotta go.*

CAIN: *K. Talk later.*

He set his phone on the dresser and gazed down at Rayna's panties, replaying last night, getting hard all over again at the way she had responded to him.

It looked like he was going to have *that* kind of shower this morning. And tonight. And tomorrow. His hand was going to stay well acquainted with his dick for months over the memories of last night.

Cain was *not* the marrying type. Never was, never would be. But if he were, Rayna would be what was called a keeper. He barely knew her, but he knew that much. He also knew she was going to make some lucky man very happy someday.

Very happy.

With a dark but approving chuckle, he set her panties on the dresser next to the note and turned for the bathroom.

It was utterly amazing to think that right now, somewhere out in the world, there was a man who had no idea what was waiting for him. That man had no idea that Rayna was his destiny. No idea he was going to propose to her. No idea how special he was because Rayna was going to tell him yes. More importantly, this man had no fucking clue how fiercely his world would be rocked when he finally met her and realized he'd found the woman he was going to marry.

But Cain did. He'd experienced just a taste of

what Rayna had to offer last night, and it had almost been enough to make him believe in the institution of marriage. Almost, but not quite. But that was more than any other woman had been able to accomplish. Before last night, Cain had never even considered marriage could be more than just a ruse you showed the world to hide who you truly were. Like his parents. Marriage was little more than window dressing for what happened when the eyes of the public weren't on them.

While he was jaded about his own beliefs about marriage, he knew others weren't as disenchanted. And he knew that when Rayna went all-in with her future husband, it was going to be epic.

But one thing her future husband would never have that Cain could claim as his forever was last night. He grinned possessively at the thought, then sobered. He'd had only one night with her, but he had a feeling it would be a long time before he didn't use it as a yardstick for other women to measure up to. From this day forward, a woman was going to have to be pretty damn fabulous to bump Rayna off the top of the pedestal.

Cain only hoped the man she ended up marrying knew how lucky he was. How fortunate. How grateful he should be that the stars had aligned to bring them together.

What Cain didn't know was just how close her future husband already was, or how much everything in his life was about to change in ways he never anticipated.

The future had been set into motion, and there was nothing he could do now to stop it. The momentum was already building like a freight train slowly pulling away from the station. Within months, that train would be careening wildly along the tracks, a collision imminent.

Last night had only been the beginning.

But every extraordinary love story has to start somewhere.

I hope you enjoyed this free introduction to the Savage Storm Series. Find out where lightning will strike next in Savage Storm, *now available. An excerpt follows.*

Rayna started to take a backward step toward the table, but Mike took her hand, stopping her.

He leaned in close, bringing his mouth to her ear. After his lips brushed her cheek—accidentally or intentionally?—he said, "Tell Cain I'll be ready to go after I take this guy's money."

Butterflies sprang to life in her belly at the touch of his lips, and she nodded, unable to speak through the knot in her throat.

He pulled away, winked, then returned to the pool table as the other guy racked the balls.

Something was off here. Way off. Nothing was making sense, and now Mike had gone and reawakened her desire for him when the last thing she needed was to be thinking naughty thoughts about anyone other than Cain.

On shaky legs, she made her way back to the table as the crack of pool balls split the air behind her.

She sat down a few feet from Cain. "Mike says he'll be ready to leave after he finishes this game."

When Cain had led her inside Hooper's two hours ago, the way the evening would end had seemed clear. With him in her bed, or her in his. Now, she still wanted to spend the night with him, but she wasn't clear on which "him" she was referring to. Cain or Mike.

How had the night come to this? Until Cain, she had never hooked up with a stranger. And, until Mike, she had never thought she would want to do something so reckless again. But now, here she was, torn, confused, and ready to throw caution to the wind.

"He likes you," Cain said matter-of-factly.

"Oh?" She averted her eyes, not wanting him to see how much she liked Mike too.

"I told you he would." He took a final drag on his cigar, then stamped it out in the ashtray. "And you like him."

"No, I—"

"You don't need to deny it."

"I'm not denying—" She cut off cold when she looked up to find Cain wearing a mischievous grin, his gaze dark and heated, as if he found this development intensely arousing.

Her voice went into lockdown. Not only did it appear that Cain didn't mind her interest in Mike, but he was actually pleased by it. Like that had been his plan all along.

He shifted closer, leaning in. "It's okay to be attracted to both of us, Rayna. There's no law that says you have to choose."

Her heart beat a wild rhythm as she replayed his words inside her head, not sure if she'd heard him right. *There's no law that says you have to choose?*

Was Cain suggesting . . .? Was he insinuating that she could have them both? And even if he was, she had never done anything like that and wasn't sure she could. A one-night stand was one thing, but what he was suggesting was something else entirely. Going home with two men was wrong.

Wasn't it?

She looked up at Mike as he sank another shot, then lifted his steady, hopeful gaze to hers.

He knew. He knew what Cain was saying to her. They had planned this. They had come here prepared to take her home with them. With *both* of them.

Her mouth fell open as heat speared straight through her center. What would it feel like to be with both men at the same time. To have a . . . a . . . *threesome*—she almost couldn't even *think* the word without whispering it inside her mind. Just the idea was perverted enough to make her blush from the top of her head to the tips of her toes. Only bad girls did stuff like that. Dirty, slutty, smutty, bad girls.

And Rayna wasn't a bad girl. Other than last New Year's Eve, she was the epitome of the girl next door. The best, cleanest, most innocent girl you could ever meet. She had maintained her virginity until she was eighteen. She had never smoked, never experimented with drugs, and never drank to the point of excess. Textbook good girl.

Now here came Cain and Mike, suggesting she do something totally absurd. Something inconceivable, unheard-of, and foolish. Something that should have had her leaping from her seat, appalled they would even propose such an idea. Instead, she was rethinking her life choices.

Not that she would have become a drug-addicted, alcoholic prostitute or a porn star if she could get a do-over, but maybe she had played her life a little *too* safely up to this point. And, sure, maybe her agoraphobia had something to do with that, but would it be so bad to get a little wild and crazy? Maybe she would even like it.

Her breathing deepened as Cain closed the space between them.

"Is that so hard to believe, Rayna?" he asked, playing his fingers through her long hair. "That you could have two men instead of one?"

"I . . ." She looked at him, then glanced back at Mike.

Was this really happening?

Cain's index finger traced the shell of her ear as he leaned closer. "That two men find you desirable enough to want to share you?"

She drew her bottom lip between her teeth and shyly bowed her head, unable to look at either of them.

Cain brushed back her hair, caressed her cheek with his lips, then whispered against her ear, "If you think what we did on New Year's Eve was good, it was nothing compared to what Storm and I can do to you together."

She drew in her breath. God, he smelled good. Like vanilla, tobacco, and spicy deodorant. She dragged in another luscious inhale of his scent as every nerve ending in her body lit up.

He tipped his forehead to her temple. "In the

note you left me the morning after our night together, you said I'd been just what you needed, right when you needed it. Can you imagine how liberated you'll feel *tomorrow* morning if you let us show you how much more there is to see?"

"I . . . uh . . ." She tried not to tremble as his lips caressed her brow.

His scruffy cheek drifted lower, scraping hers.

Closing her eyes, she let her cheek rub provocatively against his. In her mind, she was already beneath him, her legs and arms already around him, his body already rocking hard against hers.

She was barely breathing, overwhelmed by his closeness and the heat of his body burning into hers.

A soft, rumbling moan of approval rose in his throat, making her lips part on a sigh.

The chemistry between them was as she remembered. He barely had to touch her to excite her.

Would she be able to say the same of Mike?

More importantly, did she want to take the chance to find out, when she knew what to expect from Cain?

Her gaze slid to Mike's. He stood to the side of the pool table, watching her with Cain, his chest rising and falling heavily as his opponent took a shot and missed.

How could a woman choose when faced with two such fine but distinctly different prospects? She didn't want to choose, and if Cain really was suggesting what she thought he was, she wouldn't have to.

"Tell me, Rayna . . ." She held her breath as he brushed his lips over her ear. "Have you ever been fucked by two men at the same time?"

There it was. He'd said it out loud. And the raw, primal way he said *fucked* made her grateful she was seated, or she would have collapsed from the explosive weakness that shot down her legs.

"N-no." Her mouth was drier than a bowl of talcum powder.

His fingers inched up the skirt of her dress and caressed the inside of her knee.

Mike finished his game, collected his winnings, and stuffed the wad of cash in his pocket without looking at it. Then he started for the table, his gaze locked to hers with enough fire to double down on the inferno Cain had already ignited.

Cain's fingertips trailed higher, stopping midway up her inner thigh, setting off all kinds of warning bells inside her body as the invisible link between her and Mike intensified.

She held her breath.

Just as Mike reached the table, Cain kissed the patch of skin behind her ear and whispered, "Do you want to?"

Want to find out what happens next? Order Savage Storm now and find out how the story continues!

BOOKS BY DONYA LYNNE

All the King's Men Series

Rise of the Fallen

Heart of the Warrior

Micah's Calling

Rebel Obsession

Return of the Assassin

All the King's Men - The Beginning

Bound Guardian Angel

BLACK

Micah's Bride

Raven's Gift

Strong Karma Trilogy

Good Karma

Coming Back to You

Full Circle

Banger Trilogy

Choose Me

Covet Me

Cherish Me

Donya Lynne is the bestselling author of the award winning All the King's Men and Strong Karma Series and a member of Romance Writers of America. Making her home in a wooded suburb north of Indianapolis with her husband, Donya has lived in Indiana most of her life and knew at a young age she was destined to be a writer. She started writing poetry in grade school and won her first short story contest in fourth grade. In junior high, she began writing romantic stories for her friends, and by her sophomore year, she'd been dubbed Most Likely to Become a Romance Novelist. In 2012, she fulfilled her dream by publishing her first three novels. Her work has earned her two IPPYs, five eLit Awards, a USA Today Recommended Read, and numerous accolades, including two Smashwords bestsellers. When she's not writing, she can be found cheering on the Indianapolis Colts or doing her cats' bidding.

Check out my Website:

www.donyalynne.com